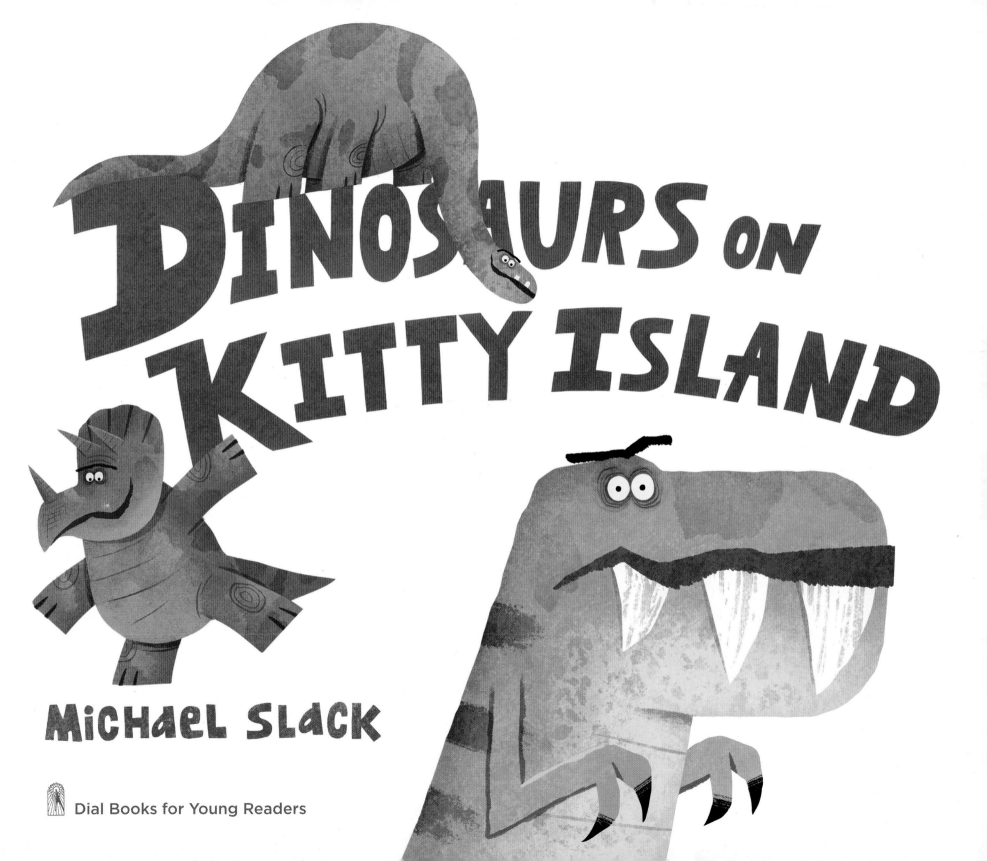

Dinosaurs on Kitty Island

Michael Slack

Dial Books for Young Readers

For Peggy Hageman

DIAL BOOKS FOR YOUNG READERS
An imprint of Penguin Random House LLC, New York

First published in the United States of America
by Dial Books for Young Readers,
an imprint of Penguin Random House LLC, 2021
Copyright © 2021 by Michael Slack

Visit us online at penguinrandomhouse.com.

Library of Congress Cataloging-in-Publication Data is available.

Manufactured in China
ISBN 9780593108413
10 9 8 7 6 5 4 3 2 1

Design by Jennifer Kelly
Text set in Gotham

The artwork was digitally painted in Photoshop.

Dinosaurs, you're bored? That's impossible! You live on Dinosaur Island.

You can . . .

Make a dirt fort.

Watch stuff sink in the tar pit.

Reassemble a skeleton.

What could be more fun than playing on Dinosaur Island?

Playing with the kitties on Kitty Island?

Dinos, that's **cuckoo pants.**

Sure, they look cute and friendly . . .
but really they are fearless and feisty.
Fun with those felines will end in catastrophe.

You do **not want** to play with those kitties.

Too late. You are going to play with the kitties.

Maybe they are taking a cat nap.
You should just let them sleep and head home.

Oh, no! They are wide-awake and ready to play.

Dinosaurs. Step away from the kitties and go back
to Dinosaur Island where it's safe.

Or . . . don't listen to me and play with these wild cats.

GAME 1:
Launch the Lizards

Well, soggysaurs, you're soaked but you survived.
A boring dirt fort sure sounds pretty great right now . . . doesn't it?

Dinosaurs?

GAME 2:
Deflate the Dirigible

Oh, dear.

This does not look like fun, dinosaurs.

You should leave before you end up as fossils.

Hold on. What are the kitties doing?

This is just embarrassing and super gross.
I have a sinking feeling this is going to end in disaster.

Dinosaurs! I know you want to be friends with these kitties.

But if you don't end this perilous playdate,
you might become **extinct!**

Another game! This is not good.
Well, it's been nice knowing you, dinosaurs.
I bet you wish you were bored now.

GAME 4:
FALL-O MEow

Even fearless furballs know when their
friends are not having fun.

TINY BABY KITTY PLAYROOM

I was wrong. You **can** have fun with the kitties on Kitty Island.
As long as everyone plays in the Tiny Baby Kitty Playroom.

Where everything is puffy, adorable, and **totally** safe.

Or not.